Note to parents, carers and teachers

Read it yourself is a series of modern stories, favourite characters and traditional tales written in a simple way for children who are learning to read. The books can be read independently or as part of a guided reading session.

Each book is carefully structured to include many high-frequency words vital for first reading. The sentences on each page are supported closely by pictures to help with understanding, and to offer lively details to talk about.

The books are graded into four levels that progressively introduce wider vocabulary and longer stories as a reader's ability and confidence grows.

Ideas for use

• Ask how your child would like to approach reading at this stage. Would he prefer to hear you read the story first, or would he like to read the story to you and see how he gets on?

• Help him to sound out any words he does not know.

• Developing readers can be concentrating so hard on the words that they sometimes don't fully grasp the meaning of what they're reading. Answering the puzzle questions on pages 46 and 47 will help with understanding.

For more information and advice on Read it yourself and book banding, visit **www.ladybird.com/readityourself**

Book Band 7

Level 3 is ideal for children who are developing reading confidence and stamina, and who are eager to read longer stories with a wider vocabulary.

Special features:

Detailed pictures for added interest and discussion

Wider vocabulary, reinforced through repetition

Simple story structure

Longer sentences

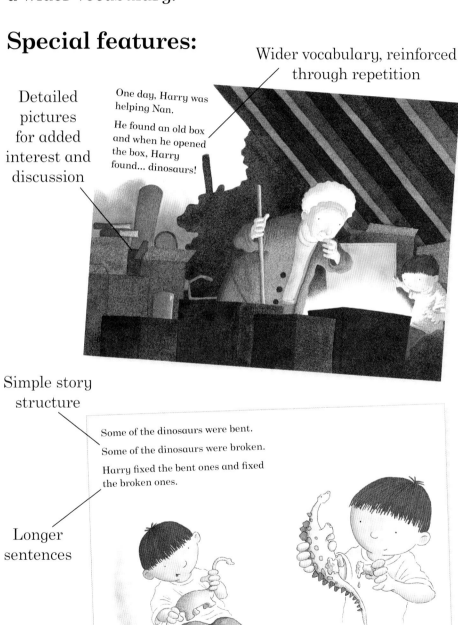

One day, Harry was helping Nan.

He found an old box and when he opened the box, Harry found... dinosaurs!

Some of the dinosaurs were bent.

Some of the dinosaurs were broken.

Harry fixed the bent ones and fixed the broken ones.

Educational Consultant: Geraldine Taylor
Book Banding Consultant: Kate Ruttle

First published by David & Charles Children's Books 1999
Text adapted by Lorraine Horsley

A catalogue record for this book is available from the British Library

This edition published by Ladybird Books Ltd
80 Strand, London, WC2R 0RL
A Penguin Company

001

Text copyright © Ian Whybrow, 2013
Illustrations copyright © Adrian Reynolds, 1999

The moral right of the author and illustrator has been asserted.

This edition produced for The Book People Ltd MMXIV.

Ladybird, Read It Yourself and the Ladybird Logo are registered or
unregistered trademarks of Ladybird Books Limited.

ISBN: 978-0-72329-374-3

Printed in China

Harry and the Bucketful of Dinosaurs

written by Ian Whybrow

illustrated by Adrian Reynolds

One day, Harry was helping Nan.

He found an old box and when he opened the box, Harry found... dinosaurs!

Some of the dinosaurs were bent.

Some of the dinosaurs were broken.

Harry fixed the bent ones and fixed the broken ones.

Then Harry took the dinosaurs
to the kitchen to wash them.

Nan came to watch.

"Dinosaurs don't like to be
shut up in boxes," said Harry.
"They like to be in a bucket."

Sam came into the kitchen.

"What is all that old junk?" she asked.

Harry was cross. "Dinosaurs are NOT old junk," he said.

The next day, Harry went to the library with Mum.

He took the dinosaurs with him in their bucket.

At the library, Harry
found a book with all
the dinosaur names in.

He said their
names to all of
his dinosaurs.

16

17

"You are my Scelidosaurus."

"You are my Stegosaurus."

"You are my Triceratops."

"You are my Tyrannosaurus."

"You are my Anchisaurus."

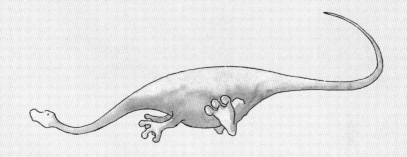

"You are my Apatosaurus."

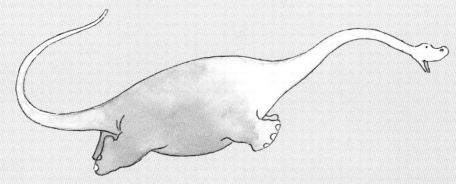

After that, the dinosaurs went everywhere with Harry.

21

When Harry had a bath,
the dinosaurs had a bath, too.

When Harry went to bed at night,
the dinosaurs went to bed, too.

When the dinosaurs got lost,
they were not lost for long.
Harry just called their names and
the dinosaurs came back to him.

One day, Harry went on a train with Nan.

He was so excited that he left the bucket of dinosaurs on the train.

Harry was very upset
and began to cry.

"Don't cry," said Nan.
"I will get you a nice
new DVD."

Harry watched the DVD with Sam.

The DVD was nice, but not as nice as the dinosaurs.

Harry was still very upset.

That night, Harry said to Mum, "I like DVDs, but I like my dinosaurs more. You can fix them and bath them and take them to bed. And best of all, you can say their names."

Harry was still upset the next day.

He got very cross when Sam said
the dinosaurs were just old junk!

Nan took Harry back to
the train station.

The man at the station
said they had found
some dinosaurs.

"But how will I know
they are your dinosaurs?"
he asked Harry.

"I will say their names," said Harry. "Then you will know."

Harry closed his eyes and called...

"Come back, my Scelidosaurus."

"Come back, my Stegosaurus."

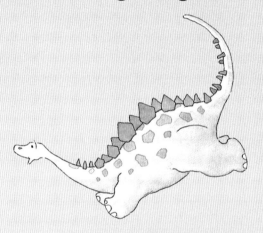

"Come back, my Triceratops."

"Come back, my Tyrannosaurus."

"Come back, my Anchisaurus."

"Come back, my Apatosaurus."

When Harry opened his eyes,
all the dinosaurs were next to
him in their bucket.

"Yes," said the man.
"These are definitely
your dinosaurs."

Harry was very excited to get all his dinosaurs back.

As they left the station, the dinosaurs all said to Harry, "We are definitely your dinosaurs and you are definitely our Harry!"

How much do you remember about the story of Harry and the Bucketful of Dinosaurs? Answer these questions and find out!

- Where does Harry find the dinosaurs?

- What does Harry keep his dinosaurs in?

- Where does Harry leave the dinosaurs?

- How does he get them back?

- Can you remember any of the dinosaur names?

Look at the different story sentences and match them to the people who said them.

"What is all that old junk?"

"You are my Stegosaurus."

"Don't cry. I will get you a nice new DVD."

"But how will I know they are your dinosaurs?"

Read it yourself with Ladybird
Tick the books you've read!

For more confident readers who can read simple stories with help.

Level 3

Longer stories for more independent, fluent readers.

Level 4